the CRiTTER club

Ellie's Spooky Surprise

by Callie Barkley ❤ illustrated by Tracy Bishop

LITTLE SIMON
New York London Toronto Sydney New Delhi

LITTLE SIMON

An imprint of Simon & Schuster Children's Publishing Division · 1230 Avenue of the Americas, New York, New York 10020 · First Little Simon paperback edition July 2023. Copyright © 2023 by Simon & Schuster, Inc. All rights reserved, including the right of reproduction in whole or in part in any form.

LITTLE SIMON is a registered trademark of Simon & Schuster, Inc., and associated colophon is a trademark of Simon & Schuster, Inc. For information about special discounts for bulk purchases, please contact Simon & Schuster Special Sales at 1-866-506-1949 or business@simonandschuster.com.

The Simon & Schuster Speakers Bureau can bring authors to your live event. For more information or to book an event contact the Simon & Schuster Speakers Bureau at 1-866-248-3049 or visit our website at www.simonspeakers.com.

Designed by Brittany Fetcho.

The text of this book was set in ITC Stone Informal Std.

Manufactured in the United States of America 0623 LAK. 10 9 8 7 6 5 4 3 2 1

Cataloging-in-Publication Data for this title is available from the Library of Congress.

ISBN 978-1-6659-2830-4 (hc)

ISBN 978-1-6659-2829-8 (pbk)

ISBN 978-1-6659-2831-1 (ebook)

Table of Contents

Chapter 1

'Tis the Spooky Season

Ellie Mitchell stepped through the swinging doors of the party store. It was a sea of orange and black. There were streamers, pumpkin cutouts, and witch hats. There were racks of costumes and shelves full of masks. Spooky music played from a speaker hidden behind a fake tombstone.

"It's the most wonderful time of the year!" Ellie exclaimed.

"It's just Halloween," said Toby, Ellie's little brother. He trailed behind Ellie, along with their mom, Mrs. Mitchell.

Ellie gasped. "*Just* Halloween?!" she cried.

Ellie adored Halloween. She had always loved dressing up. But for Halloween, everyone else dressed up too! She enjoyed seeing all the creative costumes.

Ellie also loved all the decorations. The candy aisle at the grocery store looked so festive. The mini-pumpkins lined up at the library checkout were so cute. Even the windows at school had cat and bat decals.

And then there were decorations on the houses and in the yards around Ellie's neighborhood. Including her own house! This year, Ellie was in charge of choosing their theme.

Toby went off to look at costumes. Ellie headed straight for the yard decor. There were huge fake spiders and webs to put on shrubs. There were skeletons and mummies. There were big inflatable jack-o'-lanterns.

Then Ellie saw the black cats! A whole set of cat sculptures: a big one for the lawn, one for the porch rail, and smaller cats for the windows. Each cat had an arched back and glowing eyes.

"They're perfect!" Ellie said to her mom.

Ellie could picture it: black cats climbing all over the house. She couldn't wait to set them up when she got home.

But first Ellie was going to a meeting at The Critter Club. That was the animal shelter she'd started with her friends Marion, Liz, and Amy. They were all animal lovers, like Ellie. They took care of stray animals, and did some pet-sitting too.

Their club headquarters was in their friend Ms. Sullivan's barn. Ellie's mom dropped her off there after they were done at the store. Her friends were already there.

"Ellie!" Liz cried.

Amy waved.

THE CRITTER CLUB

Marion pointed at Ellie's boot. "What's that?" Marion asked.

Ellie looked down. A piece of bright orange streamer was stuck to the bottom.

Ellie laughed. "I came from the party store," she explained. "It was *so* Halloween-y in there!"

She told her friends about the yard cats she'd picked out—and all the other decorations she'd seen.

"You really love Halloween!" Amy said with a laugh. "You always have."

Ellie nodded. "So, what do we have on the agenda for today?"

Marion looked at her clipboard. She was their unofficial club secretary because she loved to make lists and schedules.

But this week, Marion had nothing written down. She shrugged. "No pet sitting. No strays to rehome. Maybe we could organize the supply closet?"

Ellie frowned. "Ugh," she groaned. "Couldn't we do some-thing more fun?"

Amy laughed. "Like what, throw a party?" she said, joking.

Party! That was it! Ellie began to smile.

"Uh-oh," said Liz. "What are you thinking, Ellie?"

"I'm thinking Amy's exactly right," Ellie said. "We *should* throw a party. A Halloween party!"

chapter 2

Ellie's Idea

"A Halloween party?" Amy asked. "Here at The Critter Club?"

Ellie nodded. "Marion said we're not taking care of any animals this week. So it will be empty."

"I don't know," Marion replied. "We'd have to ask Ms. Sullivan."

Just then, the girls heard a familiar bark. Ms. Sullivan's dog, Rufus, came running into the barn.

"Hello, Rufus," said Amy, patting him. "Did Ms. Sullivan let you out to run around?"

Liz came over and knelt beside him. "What do you think, Rufus?" Liz asked the dog. "Should we throw a Halloween party?"

Ruff, ruff! Rufus barked and wagged his tail.

Marion laughed. "That sounds like a yes!" she said.

"I think he wants to come," Amy added.

Ellie gasped. "That's it!" she exclaimed. "Rufus *should* come! It can be a Halloween party . . . with all of our pets!"

The girls looked at one another with wide eyes. "Yes!" said Marion. "Now *that* is perfect for The Critter Club! Oh, Ollie and I would look so cute in matching costumes!" Ollie was the kitten Marion had rescued.

Amy said she'd bring her cat, Millie. Liz would bring Reggie, her ferret.

"And I'll bring Sam!" Ellie declared. He was the Mitchells' golden retriever.

Liz suggested they invite more people and pets. "How can we get the word out?" she asked.

The girls thought about this for a moment.

Amy spoke up. "A lot of pet owners come to my mom's clinic," she said. Amy's mom, Dr. Purvis, was a veterinarian. "We could put up a flyer in the waiting room."

"And one at the dog run in the park," Marion suggested.

"Or the pet food store," Liz added.

Yes! thought Ellie. With advertising, they could end up getting lots of guests!

What would Ms. Sullivan think of *that*?

"How about this?" Ellie began. "I'll go talk to Ms. Sullivan. So we can make sure she's okay with this before we get too excited."

Liz nodded. "We'll stay here and think of ideas for the flyer."

Ellie gave them a thumbs-up.

"Come on, Rufus!" she said. Rufus barked and fell into step right behind her.

Together they marched out of the barn, across the yard, and up the steps to Ms. Sullivan's front door.

Knock, knock, knock!

Ellie looked down at Rufus. Rufus looked up at her and wagged his tail.

"What do you think she'll say?" Ellie whispered.

Chapter 3

A Surprise Visitor

"Hello, Ellie!" Ms. Sullivan said as she opened the door. Rufus slipped inside and ran off down the hall. "Did Rufus interrupt your Critter Club meeting?"

"Oh, no," Ellie replied. "We love it when he joins our meetings. I just came to ask you a question."

Then Ellie explained their idea

for a Halloween pet party.

"Would it be okay if we had it in the barn?" she asked.

Ms. Sullivan's eyes lit up. "How wonderful!" she exclaimed. "Of course, Ellie! Oh, I just love costume parties. I love parties, and I love dressing up—especially in costume!" She winked at Ellie.

Right! Ms. Sullivan used to be a Hollywood actress. Not many people in Santa Vista knew that. But Ellie did. Ms. Sullivan had told Ellie when Ellie was the star in the school play. It was a special connection they had.

"I would be happy to make party snacks," Ms. Sullivan offered. "Maybe some Halloween cupcakes?"

Ellie beamed. "Thank you!" she said. "And you'll come? With Rufus?" she asked. "I mean, he sort of invited himself."

Ellie and Ms. Sullivan laughed. "We would be honored to be there," Ms. Sullivan said. "Maybe you can help us with our costumes."

Then they agreed on the best day for the party: next Saturday, the day before Halloween.

"Oh, the girls are going to be so excited!" Ellie cried. "I've got to go tell them now!"

She waved and ran off toward the barn.

Her mind raced as she ran across the grass. What could she and Sam dress up as? Something funny? Spooky? *Sparkly?* Would Sam even keep a costume on? Or would he try to wiggle out of it?

Ellie ran in through the barn door.

"Great news!" she called out. Amy, Liz, and Marion turned to face her.

Just then, Ellie stopped in her tracks.

In a flash, a small, dark, winged creature swooped within a few feet of her head.

The girls followed the shape with their eyes. Ellie tried to focus. What was it? But it was flying too fast. Her eyes couldn't quite keep up.

And for some reason, it didn't look like a bird.

It zigged and zagged and flew high up into the barn rafters.

Then it came to rest on one of the beams.

"It's hanging upside-down," Ellie pointed out.

"Um, I think I know what it is," Amy said. "I think it's . . . a *bat!*"

Chapter 4

The Bat in the Barn

"A bat?" Ellie cried out.

"What's a bat doing in here?" Marion asked. Her voice was high-pitched and strained.

"Whoa," said Liz. She sounded less nervous and more in awe. Liz was probably the one most interested in . . . unusual animals.

Amy scratched her head. "I

think bats are nocturnal. Maybe it got in overnight . . . and now it doesn't know how to get out. I hope it's okay."

They all watched the bat for a few minutes. It flew around some more. Then it returned to the beam.

Ellie nudged Amy. "Do you think your mom could come and take a look?" Ellie asked her. They definitely needed an animal expert.

Amy nodded. "Good idea," she replied. "I'll go use Ms. Sullivan's phone."

Amy headed for the door.

"I'll go with you," Marion said.

"Me too," said Liz.

Ellie turned around and followed them. "Well, I'm not staying here alone with a bat!" she declared.

Fifteen minutes later, Dr. Purvis pulled up in the driveway. The girls led her into the barn. Amy pointed up at the bat. It had moved over to another beam.

Dr. Purvis had brought binoculars so she could get a closer look. She stared through them to study the bat.

"Well, there's good news and bad news," Dr. Purvis said at last. "The good news is the bat has plenty of fur. So it's not a baby that's been separated from its mother. It's an adult and it looks healthy."

Ellie frowned. "What's the bad news?" she asked.

Dr. Purvis sighed. "I don't know the best way to set it free," she said. She explained that general vets didn't know a lot about wild animals.

Ellie's heart sank. What would they do now?

"But I have a friend who is a wildlife vet," Dr. Purvis went on. "Let me give her a call."

The girls gathered around. Amy's mom dialed her cell phone. She was on the call for a few minutes. Toward the end, Dr. Purvis was saying a lot of "uh-huh"s and "okay"s. But she *was* smiling. That had to be good, right? Ellie and the girls looked at one another hopefully.

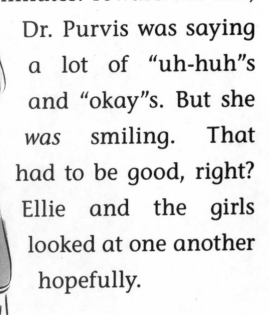

"Dr. Lane can come by tomorrow morning," Dr. Purvis said when she hung up.

"Hooray!" the girls cheered.

Amy looked up at the bat. Then she looked down at her watch. "The sun is going to set soon," she said. "Can we leave it here alone? All night long?"

Dr. Purvis nodded. "Dr. Lane suggested leaving the windows open overnight. Maybe the bat will find its way out."

So the girls went around opening the barn windows. Then they gathered their things to go. Ellie was the last one out. At the door, she looked up at the bat one more time.

Would it still be there in the morning?

49

Chapter 5

Rescue Mission

On Saturday morning, Ellie heard a scratching at her bedroom window. It shook her from sleep. The bat! Ellie sat up straight in bed. She peered out the window.

But it was just a bird, pecking on her window ledge. It flew away.

Ellie was eager to get back to The Critter Club. She hated the idea of an animal being trapped somewhere.

But there was something else, too. The sooner they freed the bat, the sooner they could plan the Halloween party!

Ellie got dressed and had break-fast. Then she got a ride with Amy and her mom over to the barn.

Ellie peeked inside the barn. Yep. The bat was still there. In almost the exact same spot. "Good morning, bat," Ellie said quietly.

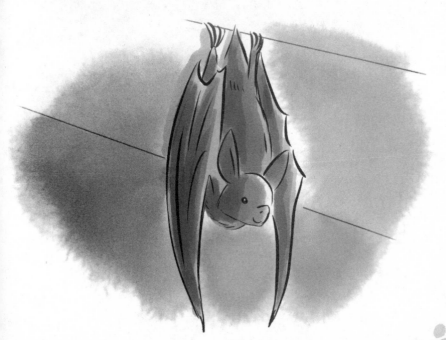

Soon all the girls were there. They watched as a van pulled up the driveway. On the side, it read CALIFORNIA FISH AND WILDLIFE.

Dr. Purvis greeted the woman who stepped out. "Thank you so much for coming!" she said. Then she introduced Dr. Lane to the girls.

"We are soooo glad you're here!" Ellie exclaimed.

They led her into the barn to see the bat.

Dr. Lane agreed with Dr. Purvis. "It is definitely an adult. A little brown bat, I think." Dr. Lane explained that was the name of a type of bat. "When did you first see it?"

"Yesterday afternoon," Marion answered. "Right around four p.m."

"It nearly flew into Ellie!" Liz added.

Dr. Lane nodded. "So it's been flying around at times?" she asked. The girls nodded.

Dr. Lane smiled. "That's a good sign," she said. "A bat that can't fly could be ill. You should never touch or pick one up." Dr. Lane said they were right to call for help. "It can be tricky to catch and release bats without hurting them," she added.

Dr. Lane went out to her van. She came back a few minutes later. She was wearing thick gloves and a hat. The hat had a net attached that covered her face.

In one hand, she had a ladder. In the other was a clear plastic container with a lid.

Ellie, Liz, Amy, Marion, and Dr. Purvis stood back to watch.

In no time at all, Dr. Lane was up the ladder. She slowly covered the bat with the container. Then she carefully slid the lid between the beam and the container.

Now the bat was inside!

Then Dr. Lane came down the ladder.

"Wow!" Liz said. "You made that look so easy!"

Dr. Lane took off her hat and smiled. "Slow and steady, that's the trick," she said. Dr. Lane took a close look at the bat through the clear plastic. "I think it's a male," she said.

Ellie was amazed by how fuzzy the bat was. And how large his ears were compared to his body.

"He's actually pretty cute," Marion said.

"Yeah," Liz agreed. "Not like a scary flying monster with fangs."

"But that would be a good name," Ellie suggested. "Fang!"

The girls all laughed and agreed.

Fang and Friends

"What now?" Dr. Purvis asked. She and the girls were following Dr. Lane back to her van.

"I'll take Fang back to our wildlife center," Dr. Lane explained. "I want to make sure he's healthy. Then he can be released. But he'll be safer from predators if he's set free after dark."

Dr. Lane gently placed the container in the back of her van.

"How about I bring Fang back later this week?" Dr. Lane asked. "You can help me release him."

"Yes!" all the girls said together.

"Okay!" Dr. Lane replied with a laugh. "And in the meantime . . ."

Dr. Lane reached into the van.

"Maybe you want to put up a bat house for Fang's friends?" she asked. Dr. Lane pulled out a wooden structure that looked like a big birdhouse.

Dr. Lane explained why bat houses are important. They offer a safe place for bats to roost, or nest.

"And that's good," Dr. Lane said. "Because bats are important little creatures. Little brown bats like this one eat a lot of mosquitos and other insects. That means farmers don't have to use so many pesticides. And *fruit-eating* bats help to spread seeds and pollinate flowers."

Dr. Lane told the group that some types of bats are endangered. "We can help them by making our yards more bat-friendly," she said.

Before she left, she told the girls that they could paint the bat house if they wanted to. And she suggested they hang it on the outside of the barn. "At least ten or fif-teen feet off the ground," Dr. Lane said.

Amy's mom nodded. "I'll make sure it's okay with Ms. Sullivan," she told the girls.

They all thanked Dr. Lane as she climbed into the van.

"Bye, Fang!" they called as the van drove away.

Then they were so excited to decorate the bat house, they got started right away. Liz pulled some paint cans out of the supply closet. "We have orange, red, blue, purple, and black," she announced.

Right away, Ellie picked up two
of the paint cans: orange and black.
"Are you thinking what I'm thinking?" Ellie asked.

"Halloween colors?" Marion
said.

Ellie nodded.

Now that Fang was safe and sound, they could start thinking about the party again. They started painting while they made plans.

"I have an idea!" said Marion. "Each of us can make a party flyer this weekend. Then, on Monday, we can hang them up in the place we've each chosen."

They agreed on the details to put on the flyers—to make sure they all had the same information. By the time they had it all figured out, they were done painting.

The bat box was orange with black bats all over it.

"Simple but spooky," Ellie declared. "I think Fang would like it."

You're Invited . . .

Ellie made sure to get to school early on Monday. She carried her flyer into the main hall. She picked out a good spot on the bulletin board, and she pinned it up.

Ellie sensed someone standing behind her. She turned to see a third-grader. "Oh, wow," he said. "A pet party?" He stopped a fourth-grader walking by. "Look at this," he said. He pointed at the flyer. "I am definitely bringing my dog. We still have her robot costume from last year."

The fourth-grader laughed. "My cat would make the perfect ballerina," she said. "Maybe we'll come!"

Ellie beamed. The flyer had been up for only one minute. She was thrilled by the reaction.

In the classroom, Ellie told Liz, "I think people are actually going to come!"

Liz clapped. She said her dad offered to hang her flyer at the pet food store.

At lunch, Amy said she'd hung hers at the vet clinic. And Marion was taking hers to the dog run after school. There was a community bulletin board by the parking lot.

As Ellie opened her soup container, she felt a tap on her shoulder. She turned. A kindergartner was looking at her with wide eyes.

"Can *anyone* come to your pet party?" he asked.

Ellie smiled. "Yes, of course!" she told him.

The kindergartner's face lit up with a huge smile. He turned and hurried back to his lunch table. Ellie could read his lips as he told his friends, *She said yes!*

"Wow!" Ellie said. "Word is getting around!"

Marion suggested they meet up at the barn after school. "We have a lot more planning to do," she pointed out. "But I do have one thing checked off: my costume."

Marion explained that she already had a pair of butterfly wings. She'd made them for a butterfly release event at the Arboretum.

"I'll make a mini version for Ollie," Marion said. "And maybe an antenna headband—if he'll keep it on his head!"

Liz laughed. "That will be so cute!" she said. "I wonder if I can make a shiny, scaly tail to fit over Reggie's ferret tail. Then we can be mermaids!"

Amy went next. "I was planning on dressing up as a detective," she told them. "So maybe Millie can be my sidekick."

Ellie frowned. Her friends had such good ideas. "I'm not sure what Sam and I are going to be," Ellie said. "What's spooky but not too hard to make?"

An image popped into Ellie's head. It was the bat house they'd painted on Saturday. Orange and covered with . . .

"Bats!" Ellie cried out. "That's it!"

Chapter 8

Party Planning

"Okay," said Marion. It was Monday afternoon at The Critter Club. "We have five days between now and Saturday. It's not too soon to start decorating!"

Ellie tapped her chin. "It's tricky that we don't know how many people will come," she said.

Amy nodded. "My mom said

that the flyer at the clinic is getting a lot of attention. Oh, and she said Dr. Lane called. Fang was a little weak, but he's getting stronger. She wants to bring him back on Saturday to release him."

"Perfect!" Ellie said. "We'll already be here for the party!"

Even though they didn't know how many guests to expect, the girls threw themselves into decorating mode.

Marion and Amy pulled out a stack of construction paper. They started making long paper chain streamers.

Liz sketched Halloween shapes onto cardboard: pumpkins, bats, and ghosts. Then Ellie cut them out and painted them different colors. They planned to hang them up around the barn.

On Tuesday after school, they talked about party games.

"We could play Pin the Tail on the Cat!" Liz suggested.

"And Musical Pumpkins!" added Ellie. "You know, Musical Chairs—only it sounds more Halloween-y!"

Marion suggested a Witch Hat Ring Toss. And Amy had the idea of having a candy hunt. "Like an Easter egg hunt, but with Halloween candy," she said.

On Wednesday, they made goodie bags for the guests. Liz's mom had gotten little things to put inside: stickers, glow sticks . . . and candy, of course!

By Thursday, they were putting the finishing touches on their costumes. Reggie's mermaid tail was finished, and Liz was almost done with hers. Ellie tried on her bat wings. Marion was decorating Ollie's mini-butterfly outfit.

Amy's detective costumes were all done, so she was working on a crown and velvet robe for Rufus. He and Ms. Sullivan were going as a king and queen.

Friday they set everything up. They hung the streamers. They decorated chairs with pumpkin cutouts for Musical Pumpkins. They hid all the candy for the candy hunt.

Then they set up the Witch Hat Ring Toss and Pin the Tail on the Cat.

"We should probably test them out," said Ellie with a giggle. So they played a couple of rounds of each.

Ms. Sullivan stopped by with a glass jar full of candy corn. "People can guess how many are inside," she explained. "Whoever is closest wins a prize."

The girls were thrilled. And Ms. Sullivan was the only one who knew the answer. So they could take a guess too!

Ellie went home tired, but excited. She smiled as her dad pulled into their driveway. The black cat sculptures lurked in the windows, on the porch, and on the grass.

Everything was ready for Halloween!

Happy Halloween!

The next time the girls saw one another, they were all in costume. They stood in the barn, admiring each other: Ellie the bat, Marion the butterfly, Amy the detective, and Liz the mermaid.

Ms. Sullivan gasped as she came in. "You all look fabulous!" she exclaimed.

She was carrying two large trays of food. She had made so many treats for the party! Spider donuts. Rice cereal treats with candy eyeballs. Monster cupcakes.

"These are amazing!" Ellie cried. "Thank you, Ms. Sullivan!"

"You're welcome," Ms. Sullivan replied. "Now I'm going to run off and get *my* costume on. See you in a bit!"

Ellie glanced around. The barn looked amazing. Now all they needed were guests.

Ellie's family was the first to arrive. Her parents and Toby brought Sam. "Oh, my little bat!" Ellie cried. She showered Sam with kisses.

Dr. Purvis arrived next with Millie. Millie's detective hat was a little big for her. But Amy and Millie looked adorable together.

Then came the Jenkins family with Liz's ferret, Reggie. Liz's big brother, Stewart, put Reggie down. Reggie tried to wriggle out of the mermaid tail, but then gave up and started sniffing the snack table.

And Marion's parents and her sister, Gabby, arrived with Ollie—Marion's baby butterfly.

And then . . . the guests just kept on coming!

The third-grader from school showed up with his robot dog.

The fourth-grader brought her ballerina cat.

The kindergartner came with his mom and dad. Their hamster was dressed as a taco!

Then Ms. Sullivan and Rufus made a grand entrance. They were queen and king of the party!

Ellie and the girls clapped and cheered.

Before long, the barn was filled with happy people and pets.

Marion organized a game of Musical Pumpkins. Amy helped little kids with Pin the Tail on the Cat. Liz gave hints to kids looking for the hidden candy.

Ellie supervised the candy corn jar. As she did, she came up with her own guess: 576. Ellie wrote it on a slip of paper with her name. Then she dropped it in the bowl.

Toward the end of the party, they had one last event: the pet costume parade. Two by two, kids and their pets paraded around the barn. Ellie and Sam led the way.

Halfway around, Ellie stepped out of line. She just wanted to watch the parade go by. Her smile was so huge, her cheeks kind of hurt. But she was so happy.

This was the best Halloween ever!

Before the guests started to leave, Ms. Sullivan made an announcement. "The number of candy corns in the jar was . . . 600! The closest guess was 576, made by Ellie!"

Ellie couldn't believe it! "I won?" she cried.

Ms. Sullivan nodded. "And here's your prize." She handed Ellie the jar.

"Good thing I love candy corn!" Ellie exclaimed.

Goodbye . . . for Now

The girls handed out goodie bags as guests said goodbye.

As cars drove off down the driveway, one van was coming in.

It was Dr. Lane! She stepped out holding Fang in the container.

"Happy Halloween!" Ellie said. "How is he?"

Dr. Lane nodded. "He's been

eating well and he seems stronger," she said. "I think he's ready to be back in the wild!"

Marion ran into the barn. She came back with the bat house to show Dr. Lane.

"I love how you painted it!" Dr. Lane said. She tapped her chin. "You know, we could use the bat house as Fang's launch pad." She turned to Ellie. "Would you hold Fang a minute?"

Ellie held the container. *Whoa,* she thought. She had never been this close to a bat before.

Dr. Lane got her ladder out of the van. She leaned it against the barn. Then she climbed up to hammer a special hanger into the siding.

Dr. Lane came down and gently took Fang from Ellie.

Then she climbed up again. This time, she opened the lid just a bit. Fang climbed out and into the bat house.

Dr. Lane came down and stood with the girls. "Watch," she whispered.

The girls watched the bat house. The moonlight cast shadows. Ellie didn't know what she was looking for, and she was pretty sure she couldn't see anything happening.

Suddenly, a shadowy figure dropped out of the bat house. Fang flapped his wings furiously. He zigged and zagged and rose up high into the night sky.

"Will he be back?" Amy asked.

Dr. Lane shrugged. "Maybe," she said. "Maybe not. But the bat house will be here for any bats that might need it."

Ellie smiled. She was glad they could help. She knew they would always remember Fang, the Halloween bat.

THE CRITTER CLUB